For Beatrice, Eva, Grace, and Willie
and Mary Jane and Jack

There was once an emperor
who loved new clothes.

He spent all of his money on clothes.
And he spent all of his time
trying on new suits and showing them off.

The
Emperor's
New Clothes

by HANS CHRISTIAN ANDERSEN

A new English version by RUTH BELOV GROSS

Pictures by JACK KENT

SCHOLASTIC INC.
New York Toronto London Auckland Sydney

ISBN 0-590-40148-3

Text copyright © 1977 by Ruth Belov Gross. Illustrations copyright © 1977 by Jack Kent. All rights reserved. Published by Scholastic Inc.

12 11 10 9 8 7 6 5 4 3 2   6 7 8 9/8 0/9

Printed in the U.S.A.   09

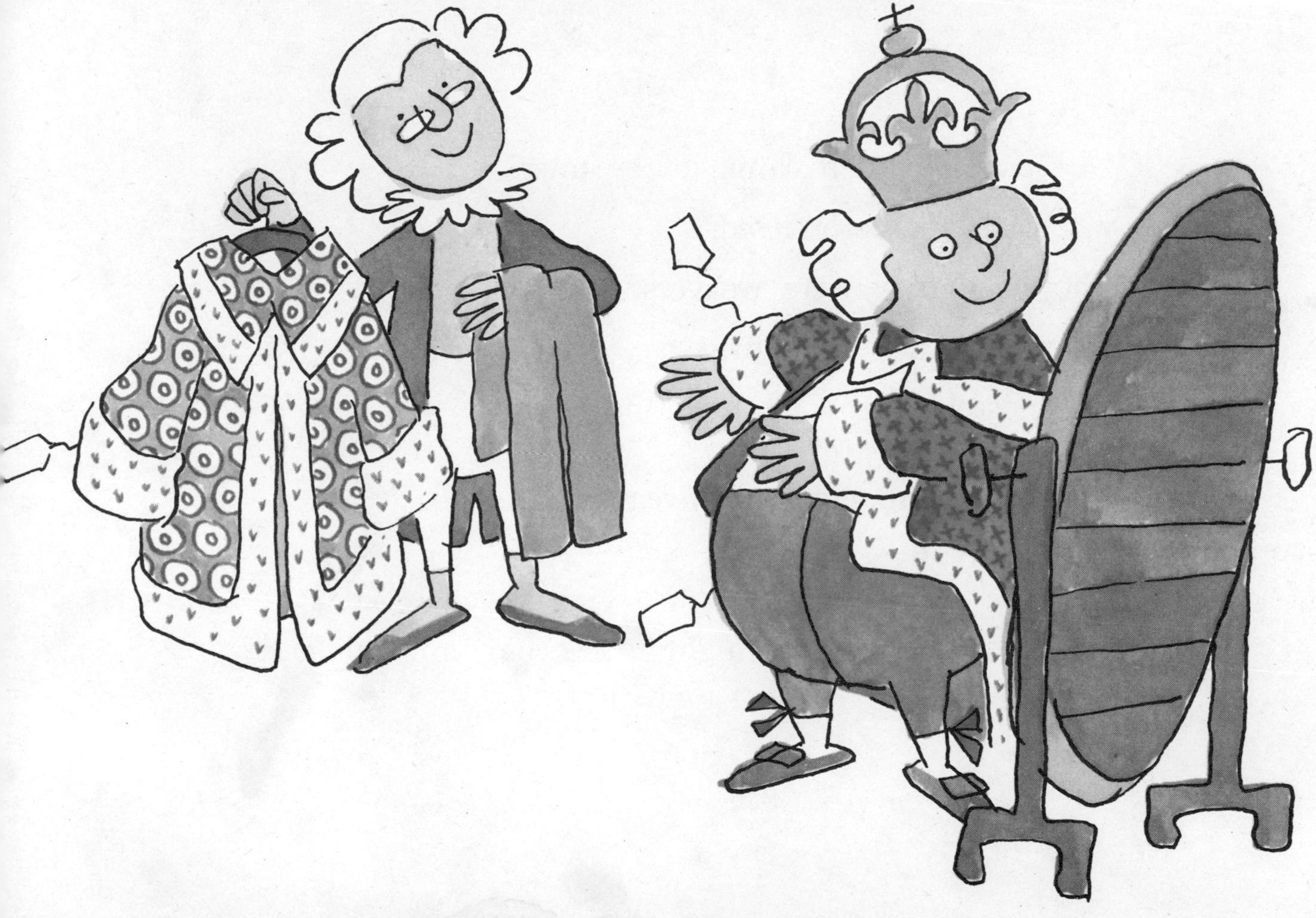

One day two men came to the town
where the emperor lived.
They said they were weavers.
They said they could weave
the most beautiful cloth in the world.

The men were not really weavers, though.
They were liars.

The two men went straight to the emperor's palace.

"Your Majesty," said one of the men,
"everybody knows about
the beautiful cloth we weave."

"But have you heard the amazing
thing about it?" the other man said.
"Some people cannot see our cloth.
They cannot see it
even when they are looking right at it."

"Cannot see it!" said the emperor.
"What kind of people
cannot see your beautiful cloth?"

"Stupid people," said one man.

"And people who are not good
at their jobs," said the other.

"That is truly amazing!" the emperor said.
"I must have a suit
made out of that cloth."

The emperor told the two men
to begin weaving the cloth at once.

The men said they would need a lot of money.
And they said they would need
the best gold thread
and the best silk thread
to weave with.

The emperor gave them the money
and the thread. And he gave them
a room in his palace
to work in.

9

The men put up two big looms to weave on.
But they did not put the thread on the looms.
They put the thread away in a bag.

Day after day,
the two men sat at the empty looms
and pretended to weave.

Everyone was waiting
for the cloth to be finished.
Everyone was waiting to find out
if their friends would be able to see it.

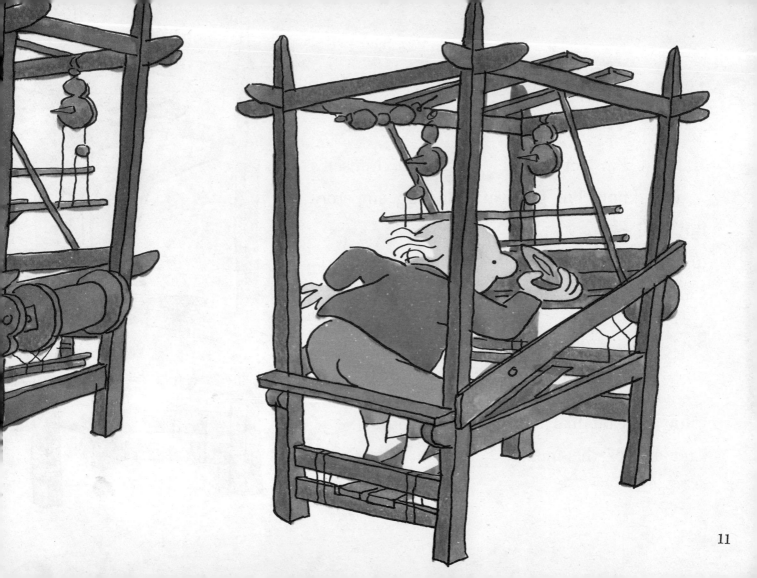

The emperor wanted to go and look at the cloth.
He was sure he would be able to see it.

"I know I'm not stupid," he said to himself.
"And I know I'm good at being an emperor.
But still —
just this once —
I think I'll send somebody else."

So the emperor sent his chief minister
down to the workroom.

"How do you like our beautiful cloth?"
said one of the men.

The chief minister looked at one loom
and then at the other.
He couldn't see any cloth,
because there wasn't any cloth to see.

"Dear me," he said to himself,

"I can't see the cloth! Am I stupid?

I never thought I was. Am I bad at my job?

If I am, I must keep it a secret.

I must not say that I cannot see the cloth."

So the chief minister said to the men,

"The cloth is beautiful."

"Be sure to tell that to the emperor,"

said one of the men.

"Tell him about the beautiful colors.

And tell him how the gold thread shines."

The chief minister went back to the emperor.

"The colors are beautiful!" he said.

"The reds! The purples!

And how the gold thread shines!"

The next day the two men
asked the emperor for more money
and more gold thread and more silk thread.

The emperor gave them the money and the thread.
The men put the money in their pockets.
They put the thread away in their bag.
And they kept on pretending to weave.

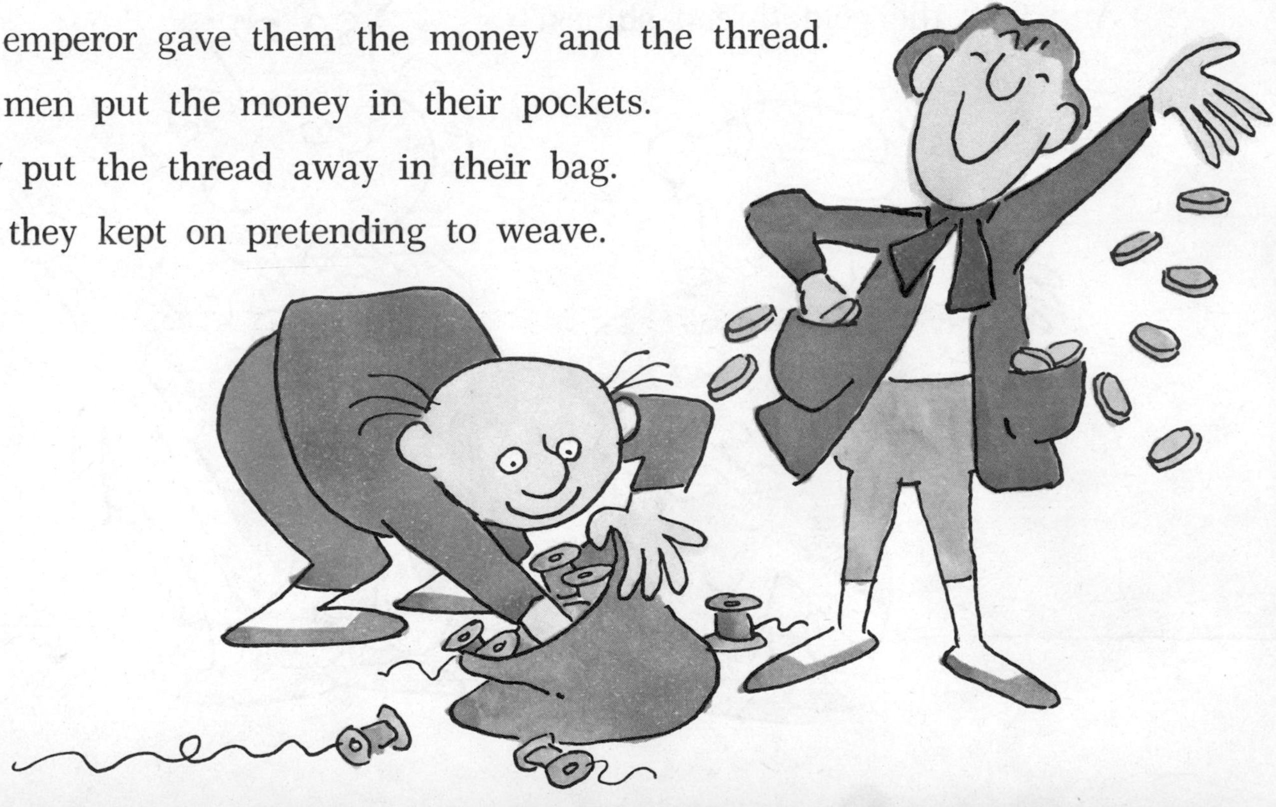

Soon the emperor wanted to know
when his cloth would be finished.
This time he sent his second chief minister
down to the workroom.

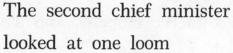

The second chief minister
looked at one loom

and then at the other.

He couldn't see a thing
on the looms,
because there wasn't a thing
to see.

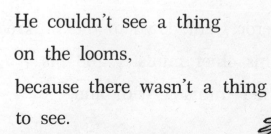

17

"Oh, dear," he thought.

"I can't see the cloth!

But I'd better pretend that I can."

So he said to the men, "The cloth is beautiful."

And he went back to the emperor and said,

"The cloth is really beautiful!"

The emperor couldn't wait a minute longer.

He had to see the beautiful cloth

for himself.

The emperor went down to the workroom.

He took his chief minister and his

second chief minister with him.

The first chief minister
looked at the empty looms.
"How the gold thread shines!"
he said.

The second chief minister said,
"The cloth is really beautiful."

The emperor looked at one loom
and then at the other.
He could not see a thing on the looms.

"What is this?" he said to himself.
"Am I stupid? No, that is not possible.
Is it possible that
I am not a good emperor?
Oh, no! That would be terrible!
Well, I will have to pretend
that I see the beautiful cloth."

So the emperor said to the two men,
"Excellent! Beautiful! Wonderful!"
And he gave each of them a medal
to show how pleased he was.

"And now, Your Majesty," said one of the men,
"we are ready to cut the cloth
and make a suit for you."

"Splendid!" the emperor said.
"We are having a big parade next week.
I will wear my new suit then."

Before the day of the parade,
the two men stayed up all night.
They used more than twenty candles
to light the room, so everyone could see
how hard they were working.

They pretended to take the cloth off the looms.
They moved their hands around in the air
and snapped their scissors together.

They used big needles
and pretended to sew with them.
But the needles had no thread.

At last it was morning —
the day of the big parade.
"And now," said one of the men,
"the emperor's new clothes are ready."

The emperor went to the workroom
at once.

One of the men pretended
to hold out a coat.
"Here is your new coat, Your Majesty,"
he said. "It is as light as a feather."

"Here are your new trousers,"
the other man said.

"And here is your long royal cape.
Your new clothes are so light,
you will hardly feel you have them on."

The emperor took off the clothes
he was wearing.
And the two men pretended to help him
put the new ones on.

The emperor turned round and round
in front of the mirror.
"My new clothes feel as light
as a feather," he said.

Two noblemen were supposed to hold up the ends
of the new royal cape.
They couldn't see the cape.
They couldn't see the trousers or the coat either,
but they weren't going to say so.

They felt around on the floor
and pretended to pick up the ends of the cape.

Then the emperor and the noblemen
marched out of the palace.

In the street the people were waiting
to see the big parade.
"Look at the emperor!" the people cried.
"What a beautiful new suit he has!"

Nobody could see the emperor's new clothes.
But nobody was going to say so.
"Look at the emperor!" everybody said.
"What a beautiful new suit he is wearing!"

"He hasn't got anything on!"
a little child said.

"Did you hear what that child said?"
somebody whispered.
"A little child said that the emperor
hasn't got anything on!"

"Hasn't got anything on!"
One person said it,
and then another,
and another.

"Hasn't got anything on!"
everybody shouted at last.
"The emperor hasn't got anything on!"

The emperor knew now
that the people were right.
But he had to stay in the parade
until it was over.

"The parade must go on,"
the emperor thought,
"and I must keep going too."

So the emperor walked proudly
the rest of the way.

And the two noblemen walked behind him,
holding up the ends of the new royal cape —

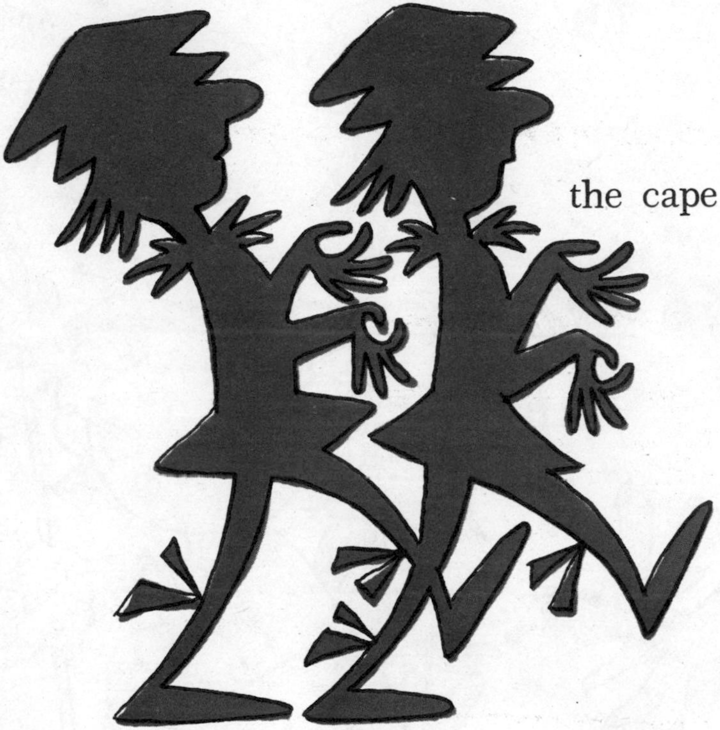

the cape

that

wasn't there.

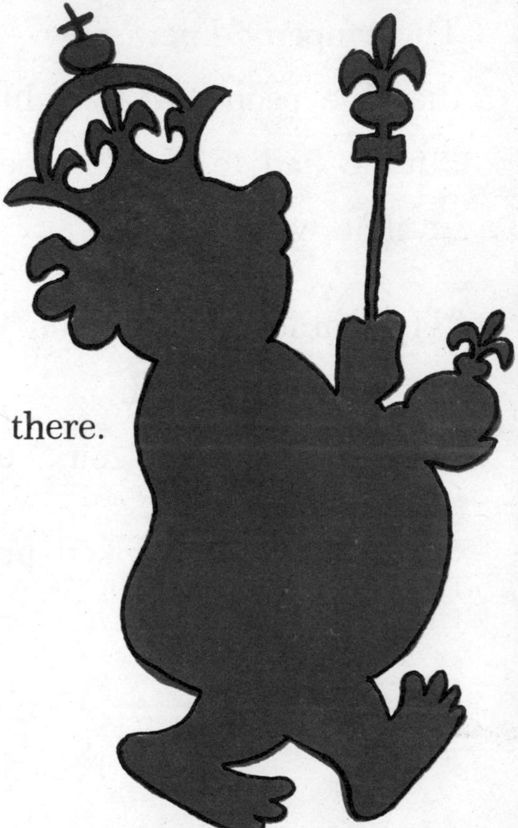